BANDED
SEA KRAIT

by Craig Boutland

Consultant: Chris Mattison, herpetologist

BEARPORT
PUBLISHING

Minneapolis, Minnesota

Credits

Cover, ©Rich Carey/Shutterstock; 1, ©Rich Carey/Shuttertock; 3, ©Rich Carey/Shutterstock; 4, ©Orlandin/Dreamstime; 5, ©Rich Carey/Shutterstock; 7, ©Ethan Daniels/Shutterstock; 7BR, Elias Levy/ Public Domain; ©8, ©Jack Pokoj/Shutterstock; 9, ©Greens and Blues/Shutterstock; 10, ©Matt9122/ Shutterstock; 11, ©Ethan Daniels/Shutterstock; 12L, ©Skef1964/Dreamstime; 12R, ©nartt/Shutterstock; 13, ©Rich Carey/Shutterstock; 14, ©Ethan Daniels/Shutterstock; 15, ©Gerals Cubitt/Avalon; 16, ©Bernhard DUPONT from France/Public Domain; 17, © Ethan Daniels/Shutterstock; 18, ©Norjipin Saidi/ Shutterstock; 19, ©Hemis/Alamy; 20, ©Tobias Bernhard/NHPA/Photoshot/Avalon; 21, ©Damsea/ Shutterstock; 22TL, © Ingrid Pakats/Shutterstock; 22R, ©Nick Hobgood/Public Domain; 22BL, ©Davic Sandford/Dreamstime; 23, ©Rich Carey/Shutterstock; 24, © Rich Carey/Shutterstock.

T=Top, B=Bottom, L=Left, R=Right

President: Jen Jenson
Director of Product Development: Spencer Brinker
Editor: Allison Juda
Designer: Micah Edel
Editorial and Design: Brown Bear Books Ltd
Brown Bear Books has made every attempt to contact the copyright holders.
If anyone has any information please contact licensing@brownbearbooks.co.uk

Library of Congress Cataloging-in-Publication Data

Names: Boutland, Craig, author.
Title: Banded sea krait / by Craig Boutland.
Description: Minneapolis, Minnesota : Bearport Publishing Company, [2021] |
  Series: Slither! | Includes bibliographical references and index.
Identifiers: LCCN 2020018888 (print) | LCCN 2020018889 (ebook) | ISBN
  9781647470937 (library binding) | ISBN 9781647471026 (paperback) | ISBN
  9781647471118 (ebook)
Subjects: LCSH: Sea kraits--Juvenile literature.
Classification: LCC QL666.O64 B68 2021 (print) | LCC QL666.O64 (ebook) |
  DDC 597.96--dc23
LC record available at https://lccn.loc.gov/2020018888
LC ebook record available at https://lccn.loc.gov/2020018889

For more information, write to Bearport Publishing, 5357 Penn Avenue South, Minneapolis, MN 55419. Printed in the United States of America.

Contents

Snake in the Water

A long, thin animal swims with the fish near a colorful **coral reef**. But this animal doesn't have gills or fins. It's a snake!

Unlike most snakes, banded sea kraits spend most of their lives in the ocean. But like many other snakes, they are **venomous**. A bite from a banded sea krait has enough **venom** to kill 12 people.

These snakes hardly ever bite people and are more likely to swim away when people are near.

Built for the Ocean

The banded sea krait can be found in the warm, shallow waters of the Indian and Pacific oceans. Its body has special **adaptations** that help it survive in the water. A **gland** under its tongue gets rid of extra salt that enters the snake's body from the ocean water around it. And its lungs are bigger than those of land snakes. This is so the snaky swimmer can hold its breath under water. The snake's tail is shaped like a paddle to push the snake through the water.

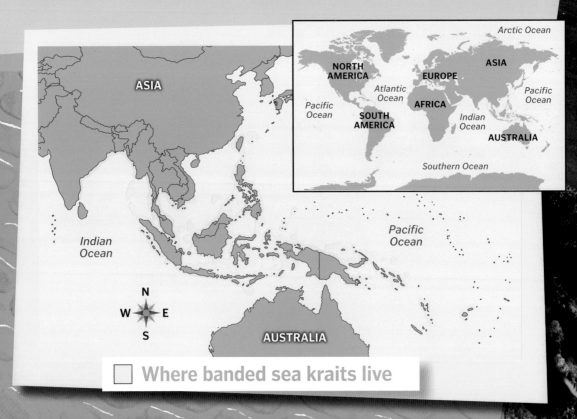

Where banded sea kraits live

Unlike fish, banded sea kraits can't breathe underwater. They have to come to the surface to breathe.

A sea krait's paddle-shaped tail

What's in a Name?

Banded sea kraits are hard to miss as they swim through the water. Female banded sea kraits can grow up to 4.2 feet (1.3 m) long, while the males can be up to 2.5 ft (0.8 m) in length.

Striking black bands on light blue or gray bodies give the snakes their name. These bands warn other animals that the snake is venomous.

The banded sea krait has a yellow upper lip. This gives the snake its other common name—the yellow-lipped sea krait.

Heads or Tails?

Despite stripes that warn of powerful venom, banded sea kraits still have **predators**. Sea eagles snatch them from the surface of the ocean or when they make their trips to land. Sharks hunt them in deeper water. But the snakes have a special way to trick enemies. Banded sea krait tails look just like the snakes' heads. This might fool predators into thinking they are facing heads with deadly venom rather than harmless tails!

A tiger shark

The snake moves its tail in the same way as it moves its head. This helps to trick predators.

11

On the Menu

Banded sea kraits hunt in the ocean. They mainly eat eels. But male and female kraits hunt different **species** of eels, so they avoid competing for food. Female sea kraits eat larger conger eels that live in deep ocean waters. The male snakes hunt smaller moray eels in shallow waters.

A moray eel

A conger eel

Banded sea kraits can dive down to about 330 ft (100 m) when they hunt.

A Deadly Bite

When a banded sea krait hunts, it swims slowly over coral reefs, poking its head into holes to look for **prey**. When the snake spots its victim, it bites. The sea krait's **fangs** inject deadly venom into the creature. This stops the victim's muscles from working. Once the prey is dead, the snake swallows it whole.

A sea krait swims over a coral reef looking for food.

Sometimes the snake bites its victim and holds on until the venom works. Other times, it lets its prey go and follows until the creature dies.

An eel

Snakes Ashore

After the snake has eaten, it is heavy and slow in the water. It goes onto land to **digest** its meal. The snake will hide under rocks or in holes along the shores of small islands near its watery home. The banded sea krait also comes onto land to **shed** its skin and to **mate**.

Banded sea kraits have large **scales** on their bellies that help them move on land.

Time to Mate

When it is time to mate, male snakes gather in the shallow water near the coast and wait for females to arrive. The female snakes go onto land first. Male snakes follow a special scent trail to find the females. After mating, the snakes stay on land for several hours. Then, they go back into the sea.

Two banded sea kraits mating

Banded sea kraits return to the land where they were born when they are ready to mate. They might travel long distances to get there.

Beach Babies

When she is ready to lay her eggs, the female snake comes back to the same beach. She lays her eggs on the sand or in a cave. There, they develop for about four months. Then, the eggs hatch and the baby snakes head to the ocean. In another two years, the banded sea kraits are ready to have their own snake babies.

Young banded sea kraits spend less time on land than adult sea kraits.

Banded Sea Krait Facts

Banded sea kraits come to land to shed their skin every two to six weeks.

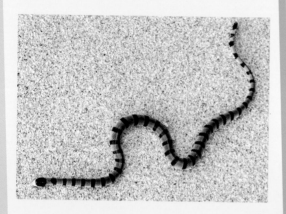

Female sea kraits lay between 4 and 10 eggs at a time.

An eel called the banded snake eel looks just like the banded sea krait. The disguise tricks predators into thinking the harmless eel is a venomous snake so they leave the eel alone.

A banded snake eel

There are eight species of sea kraits. The others include the blue-banded sea krait and the Rennel Island sea krait.

A blue-banded sea krait

Banded sea kraits move five times faster in the water than on land.

Glossary

adaptations special skills or parts of the body that help an animal survive

coral reef an underwater structure made from the bodies of animals called corals

digest to break down food inside the body

fangs pointed teeth

gland a part of the body that makes a useful substance or does a useful job

mate to come together to have young

predators animals that hunt and kill other animals for food

prey animals that are hunted and killed by other animals

scales tough, waterproof coverings on a snake's body

shed to lose a layer

species groups that animals are divided into, according to similar characteristics

venom poison from a snake that is injected through fangs

venomous an animal that has venon

Index

Read More

George, Gale. *Sea Snakes (Snakes on the Hunt).* New York: PowerKids Press (2017).

Pettiford, Rebecca. *Coral Reef Food Chains (Who Eats What?).* Minneapolis: Jump! (2017).

Terp, Gail. *Sea Snakes (Bolt. Super Sea Creatures).* Mankato, MN: Black Rabbit Books (2021).

Learn More Online

1. Go to **factsurfer.com**
2. Enter "**Sea Krait**" into the search box.
3. Click on the cover of the book to see a list of websites.

About the Author

Craig Boutland has written many science,
history, and nature books for children.
He divides his time between London
and the English countryside.